KARLO'S TALE

Karlo is miserable when he discovers that he is the only child to be left behind when the Pied Piper takes all the other children away. He becomes even more cast down when he realizes that he must rescue the children – but cheers up considerably when he makes friends with a very brave and clever rat, named Josefina, who promises to help him.

Also available by Robert Leeson

Wheel of Danger
Challenge in the Dark
The Demon Bike Rider
Right Royal Kidnap
Hey, Robin!
The Reversible Giant

KARLO'S TALE

Young Lions
An Imprint of HarperCollinsPublishers

For Judy

First published in Young Lions in 1993

Young Lions is an imprint of CollinsChildren'sBooks,
part of HarperCollins*Publishers* Ltd
77-85 Fulham Palace Road, Hammersmith,
London, W6 8JB

5 7 9 10 8 6

Text copyright © Robert Leeson 1993
Illustrations copyright © Hilda Offen 1993

ISBN 0 00 674320-X

The author asserts the moral right to
be identified as the author of the work.

Printed and bound in Great Britain by
Caledonian International Book Manufacturing Ltd,
Glasgow G64

ROBERT LEESON
KARLO'S TALE

ILLUSTRATED BY HILDA OFFEN

KARLO

There was once a town, a fine town, and it sat very snugly between a river and a hill.

The town was full of folk – all busy: the Mayor, the Bishop, the Teacher, the Cobbler, fathers and mothers, uncles and aunts.
For all that, it was a very quiet town. At times it was almost silent.

Something strange had happened.

All the children had gone – but one.

Each day the school bell rang for morning lessons. The Teacher waited at the gate. The Cobbler watched through his shop window, while he worked on a small pair of clogs.

They were waiting for the last child in the town, a lame boy. The Cobbler had made special wooden shoes to help him walk, slowly, but proud and straight. His name was Karlo.

And this is his story.

THE VANISHING CHILDREN

The month before, the town was plagued with
rats, bolder than dogs, quicker than cats.
People were at their wits' end.

Even the Mayor, smart as he was in his red
robe and his gold chain, did not know what to
do. The town was in despair.

Then one day a strange man arrived,
dressed in red and yellow and carrying a pipe.

He announced:

"For a thousand pounds I'll play your rats away."

"Go ahead," said the Mayor. A thousand, fifty thousand, what did it matter? The task was impossible.

But it wasn't. The Piper played a juicy tune, a roast beef and ripe cheese tune. In a trice, all the rats poured into the streets and down to the river where they fell in and drowned.

The townsfolk were amazed. But the Mayor's crafty mind worked quickly. Why pay as much as a thousand pounds when all the rats were dead? "Here's fifty pounds," he told the man in red and yellow.

Furiously, the Piper answered. "I have done my work. Why try to trick me out of my pay? Is money so important to you?"

"Nothing is more important in this life, my

friend," laughed the Mayor.

"Well," said the Piper. "Let's see if that's true."

Once more he played, a tune of sunshine, games and laughter. Now to the horror of the people every boy and girl followed the Piper to the hill behind the town.

Karlo went too, but lagged behind. He could hear the other children singing:

"No more parents, no more school
We shall live a life of ease.
No more going by the rule,
We shall do just as we please."

Suddenly, with a noise like thunder, the mountain which loomed over the town and lay well beyond the river, opened wide. Singing and dancing, the children followed the Piper inside. But just as Karlo arrived the rock wall closed, and he was left alone.

KARLO FOR SALE

A meeting was called in the Town Hall.
Everyone came. The Mayor said, gravely:
"My friends. We are not alone. I am told that
this rogue is going from town to town,
stealing children."

Angrily the Cobbler shouted: "You are the
rogue. You should have paid the Piper."

Some called out: "Hear, hear." Calmly the
Mayor raised his hand:
"What? Pay a thousand pounds to a tramp
with a penny whistle? If you were in charge,
Mr Cobbler, the town would be bankrupt.
We'd have to double the taxes."

People looked alarmed. No one wanted that.
The Teacher spoke: "So that's it? You love
money more than your children?"

"Nonsense," retorted the Mayor. "But love
won't bring them back. Neither will moaning.
They are gone."

He said cunningly: "Make the best of it. Parents are now free to do as they please. Old folk can have a nap without youngsters howling outside the window. No more rows between neighbours about their children. No more sticky fingers on shop goods. No more rude words on walls. A quiet, well-behaved town, in fact."

While people in the hall argued with each other, the Mayor went on: "Miss Teacher. You said you had too many children in each class. Now you've only one pupil."

Some laughed at that. A man called out: "Let's close the school and save more money."

The Teacher was horrified: "What about Karlo?"

"Aha," beamed the Mayor. "We will kill two birds with one stone. Any family without a child can hire Karlo for a day or a week. He'll be cared for. And the money will pay for his schooling."

Now the hall was quiet. The Mayor was so smart, he'd silenced everyone.

ENTER JOSEFINA

Karlo's new life began. Some parents wept over him. Some fed him sweets and cake. Some made him do all the work. But he didn't complain.

For Karlo had made his mind up. As soon as he could, he'd set out to find the magic land where the Piper had taken the other children.

"When I get there," thought Karlo, "my leg will be healed, I know. Then I'll do what I please."

So life went on, until something very strange happened.

Every day, Karlo saved a piece of cake from tea to eat if he felt hungry after he'd gone to bed. One night he woke and looked for his cake, but – to his surprise – it had gone!

Perhaps he'd eaten it and forgotten. But the

next night, the same thing happened. The third night he kept watch.

There, in the candle light, he saw two bright eyes, a long nose, whiskers. A rat!

But the rat did not bolt. Instead, to Karlo's amazement, it spoke.

"I'm sorry, Karlo. It's your favourite cake, but it's mine too. Now we're both alone, perhaps we can share."

"But I thought all you rats drowned," gasped Karlo.

"On no. You see, I'm Josefina, from the town down the road. When the Piper went there all the rats drowned except me. I came here and when I heard that pipe again, I warned the others to ignore it. But they thought they were bound for the Land of Heart's Desire, with honey flowing in the rivers and cheeses hanging from the trees. Instead, they drowned. You and I, Karlo, are in the same boat, let's be friends."

Karlo agreed. Josefina, or Jo, as he called her, was right. From then on he went round with his new friend tucked inside his hat or his shirt. She was safe, he had company. It was all very fine.

But it did not last.

KARLO GOES TO JAIL

One Sunday afternoon, Karlo was invited to tea at the Bishop's house. It was a magnificent spread, with trifle, jelly and ice cream, and Jo's favourite, sugar cake. The smell of it was too much for her. She popped her head out from Karlo's shirt, right in the Bishop's face.

There was pandemonium. The Bishop's wife turned green. A servant fainted. The Bishop roared: "Catch it."

Josefina escaped. But Karlo couldn't. Next morning he appeared in court in front of the Mayor.

"Keeping rats?" said the Mayor. "That's twenty years in jail, at least."

"Be merciful," said the Teacher. "He's young, and lame."

The Mayor banged on his desk with the gavel.

"He's young, is he? Then he has time to serve the full prison term. He's lame, eh? In jail he won't have to walk at all. But I'm a reasonable man. Since it's a first offence I'll knock off two weeks. Now lock him up."

JO TO THE RESCUE

That night, poor Karlo lay down in the straw
on his cell floor and tried to sleep. But it was
no use. Twenty years? – his life would be
almost over by the time he was free again.
He'd be nearly thirty. And now he would
never find the Land of Heart's Desire where
the Piper had led the children.

As he tossed and turned, something tugged
at his sleeve. A second later, another gentle
tug. Then came a quiet voice in his ear.

"Karlo, love. It's Josefina."

"Oh, you," said Karlo grumpily. "You ran
away. See where you landed me."

"I know," squeaked Jo soothingly. "I'm
sorry. Now I've come to take you away."

"Away? How?" demanded Karlo. "You can
come and go as you like. I'm stuck."

"Not a bit," answered Jo. "A rat will never
forsake a sister or brother. You are as good as

a rat any day. So, on your feet and follow me."

In the corner of the cell, under filthy straw, was a grating. When Karlo pulled it up, the stench from below almost choked him. But Jo had disappeared down the opening.

"Come on, Karlo," she called. "It leads to the river."

"But it's the sewer!"

"I daresay. We shan't smell like roses. But we shall be free. Come on."

And in the morning, when the jailer came, the cell was empty. Jo and Karlo were miles away.

NO CHILDREN LEFT

With Karlo gone, the town had no children left at all.

They were missed more and more. Mothers and fathers would wake at night, thinking they heard footsteps on the stairs – but no one was there. Old folk, who used to grumble about noisy boys and girls, could not sleep for worrying about where they were.

One man told the Mayor: "You are not as clever as I thought. You couldn't even keep one lame boy in jail."

"Yes," growled the Cobbler. "The cell's empty. Now there's room for someone else."

The Mayor turned pale. He knew what the Cobbler meant.

"My friends," he said. "Let us welcome children to our town from anywhere in the world."

But the people didn't know the Mayor was

only talking to save his skin. There were no children left in all the world. The Piper had taken every one.

But where?

THE JOURNEY

Karlo and Jo travelled towards the rising sun.
People on the road were kind to the lonely
boy. And rats are never at a loss for a square
meal.

They followed the Piper's trail. Karlo hoped
one day to catch up with him and join the
other children in the Land of Heart's Desire.
Josefina had something much simpler on her
mind. She just wanted to meet another rat.

Both journeyed on in hope, but at first both
were disappointed. Every town or city they
came to had lost both children and rats. And
everywhere the same thing happened – the
city guards wanted to welcome Karlo in and
keep Jo out.

Karlo would say, "No thank you," and the
two marched on. Summer moved on into
autumn. And the trail of the Piper grew
warmer.

At first they heard: "He came a month ago." Then it was a week. And later, as winter neared, they learned that they were only a day behind.

Now the bleak mountains loomed before them. Only one more town was left. And that morning, as they came in sight of the walls, they heard the sweet sound of the pipe, of running feet, shrill cries, shouting, and singing.

Karlo and Jo hurried forward. But they were still too late. Rats and children were all gone. The man in red and yellow had vanished too. There was no one to be seen.

Suddenly Jo cried out. In the river something was struggling. Boldly Karlo plunged in, and brought a half-drowned rat to shore.

"Karlo, you angel," squeaked Jo. "It's a boy."

JOURNEY'S END

The boy rat's name was Mortimer. Karlo
christened him Mo. One more
companion for the journey, he
thought.

But to his disappointment, Jo and
Mo said:

"We'll stay here. Take our
advice – stay here too. Don't
believe this dream.
Remember what the Piper
did to the other rats."

Karlo shook his head.
Somewhere beyond
those mountains he
knew he would
find all the friends
he could wish for
and he was sure

his
lame leg
would be
healed, too.
On he went. The
way grew steeper,
narrower. The sky
loomed cruel, grey and
wintry. Bitter cold wrapped him
round, white mist cut off all sight
and sound. His feet on the rough track
plunged deeper in snow.

At last he could neither go forward nor turn
back. There seemed no day nor night, no past
nor future, only empty whiteness.

He longed to rest.

The ground beneath, the sky above
vanished. He fell, fell, fell, his mind empty,
his heart numb.

THE MAGIC LAND

Karlo awoke. He heard a gentle breeze murmur in the branches of trees, and the wash of waves on a nearby shore. Then the sound of children's voices.

He opened his eyes. Gentle sunlight filled them. He sat up. Green grass rolled away to forests and hills. Close by were yellow sands and rippling water. In the distance, sails and tiny islands shimmered.

Everywhere boys and girls were playing, thousands of them. It seemed that all the children in the world were here. He had found the land he was seeking, at last.

He jumped to his feet, heart beating. Now he'd run and jump and play! But no, his lame foot dragged. He stumbled and heard laughter.

"Look how he's walking! Isn't it funny?"

Karlo fell. Grinning faces looked down on

him. Angrily, he struggled up.

"Look, he's gone red. He's funny."

Karlo shouted at them, his voice raw with rage.

They laughed even more. One asked: "Why does he fall over and shout like that?"

An older child answered: "He must like it. Why else would he do it?"

"Let's try it. All shout, all fall down," they chanted, prancing round him. Furiously, he rushed at the nearest. They scattered, shrieking with laughter.

"Catch us if you can!"

Then, just as suddenly, they stopped.

"This is boring. Let's go," they shouted.

Left alone, Karlo sat down, sick at heart. Here he was in the Land of Heart's Desire. But his leg was still lame. The other children grew bored of taunting him, and left him.

He felt hungry. To his amazement, the branches above him bent down, offering peaches, pears and oranges. He ate till he could eat no more.

In the distance, he heard the notes of a pipe. It soothed him to sleep.

SAND-CASTLES

Suddenly Karlo awoke. It was dark and the moon touched the waves with silver, though the air was soft and warm. Everything seemed so peaceful. Yet as he listened, he could hear a strange sound. He listened again. Nearby, a child was crying and whispering:
"I'm afraid."

"What's wrong?" asked Karlo.

"The Piper isn't playing. Will he ever play again? Will we ever see the sun?"

The voice was so sad. And Karlo understood sadness. He reached out, touched a small hand and stroked it.

"Sleep," he whispered. "The sun will come again."

"How do you know?"

Karlo thought.

"Because it must. It has to," he said firmly.

Morning came and the Piper played.

Laughing, shouting boys and girls scattered, all their night fears forgotten. None of them paid any attention to Karlo as he limped to and fro.

On the shore he watched children making sand-castles, with high towers, decked with coloured shells. But before each castle was complete, a mob of other children charged along the beach screaming and smashing everything down.

"What did you do that for?" shouted Karlo. They stared at him.

"Because we wanted to. Why else?"

Off they ran, while the castle builders began again as if nothing had happened. Now it was Karlo's turn to stare.

But, later, in the night he woke and heard a child cry out, "My castle's gone."

"You can make another tomorrow," comforted Karlo.

"But will the Piper play?"

"The sun will rise, Piper or no Piper," he answered.

THE HUNTERS

The next day, Karlo left the shore and wandered in the cool green shade of the woods. Nothing could go wrong here, he thought.

As he walked he heard a fearful sound. A white-faced child ran in terror down the forest track, chased by a crowd of bigger boys. They drew nearer, waving sticks, and howling ferociously as though they were a pack of hounds.

This time, Karlo didn't stop to ask why. He planted himself in front of the hunters. Facing them, he shouted, "Touch that child, and I'll kick you with my clogs."

Jeering, they came forward. Karlo struck once, twice, three times and the bullies fled, howling.

Shaking his head, he went back to the orchard where he liked to lie in the afternoon.

The hunted child walked with him.

That night the child lay by his side. But in the night he woke and wailed: "Will I see another day?" Karlo sighed. "Lie still," he whispered. "Hear my story." And he began.

"There was a town that sat so still
Between a river and a hill
A quieter spot you never spied
So calm, so peaceful, you'd have said
That all the folk had stayed in bed..."

As he told the tale of the town without

children, his small friend lay still and listened. And Karlo knew that in the darkness, others listened too.

Then the child asked, "Are all the towns like that?"

Karlo answered: "There's a whole world without children. And a world where only children live."

The child said no more.

FOLLOW THE MUSIC

The next day Karlo and his new friend sat eating fruit in the orchard. His companion looked at him and asked:

"Why are you sad? Is it because you do not walk like the others? What does it matter, when you are so brave?"

"How can I tell you what it means not to have what you long for?" Karlo replied.

His friend was puzzled. "But in this land the Piper gives everyone their heart's desire. Just ask him."

"How do I do that?"

The child smiled: "Follow the music."

Karlo stood up and walked towards the piping. He seemed to have taken only a few steps when he found himself in a shady courtyard. On a mossy wall sat the Piper, red and yellow legs crossed, pipe to his lips. Laying his pipe aside, the Piper beckoned him closer.

"Well, lame boy, what do you want?"

THE PIPER'S SECRET

Karlo gritted his teeth and asked: "Why will my leg not get better?"

"Why, my friend? Because you do not obey the laws of this land."

"Laws?" Karlo was puzzled.

"Yes. First you must forget. Yesterday brings sorrow, tomorrow, fear. Live for today. Sleep at night and don't tell stories. Stories," the Piper went on, "are memories which talk, a bridge from yesterday to tomorrow. Stories are about growing up."

He gripped Karlo's shoulder.

"So, no memories, no stories. Second. Leave others to enjoy themselves as they please, even if you think they are wicked. Here there is no right nor wrong. No past nor future. When you understand that all will be well."

The Piper's eyes gleamed like cold stars.

"Choose!"

"Choose?"

"Yes. If your leg heals, you must stay. I give everyone, parents, children, what they ask. But what they wish, can't be undone. I never let go."

Karlo's heart froze.

"You turn pale," smiled the Piper. "Fear not. You are free to limp away over the mountains again. But," he added and the smile vanished, "these children believe I make the sun rise and set. They are mine now. Take one child with you when you go, and I'll have your blood."

Karlo faced the Piper: "Suppose they wish to go as well. Can't they do as they please?"

The Piper smiled once more, but grimly this time. "Don't be too smart, lame boy."

Lifting his pipe, he played again, and Karlo found himself back in the orchard.

A LAST STORY

Karlo knew now that he couldn't stay. That night, near dawn, the children lay awake listening to his story. Then he told them, while waves broke on the moonlit shore.

"This is the last time."

"Oh, Karlo," they protested. "Why?"

"Tomorrow, when night comes, I'll leave this land and go through the mountains to the town between the river and the hill."

"Where is this town?" they asked.

"This town is anywhere and everywhere. My home and your home too, where your parents wait for you."

"For us?"

"Mothers and fathers wait, who'll hold your hand and tell you stories in the fearful night." He knew this wasn't always true but hoped that one day it might be.

"Every night, when darkness comes?" they asked.

"Oh yes. And when morning comes, you go to school, then run outside and play the fool. Each day is different, some good, some bad."

An older child said:

"There's no land beyond the mountains. Only mist and dark, because the Piper does not play there."

All were silent a moment, in fear. Then Karlo began to sing:

> *"There is a land of sunshine and of*
> *snow*
> *A land of pleasure and of woe*
> *A world of comfort and of fears*
> *A world of laughter and of tears*
> *A world of joy, a world of sorrow*
> *A world of yesterday, tomorrow."*

"Can we come with you?" his small friend asked.

Karlo shook his head. "No. I must go alone."

KARLO SETS OUT

Day came, the Piper played and Karlo
watched the boys and girls run to play. He felt
sad at the thought of leaving them, but his
mind was made up.

When the silent night came down again
he took a stick and stepped out through
the curtain of the dark towards the
steep way up into the mountain.

But as he walked he heard a quiet
voice behind him.

"Karlo, I love you. Let me go
with you."

Karlo sighed. He should
say "no" but hadn't the
heart. Reaching back
with his hand, he
said:

"Hold fast and
follow."

They
climbed
together. But
they were not
alone. Behind came
one child, then
another. Each one joined
hands and in an unending
chain they moved slowly up the
track until the mist closed round
them. They shivered as they
marched, but clung to one another,
coming by hundreds and by thousands.

At last they passed through the mist, but still
they could not see their way.

"Karlo," they wailed. "It's night here.
Endless night. We'll never see the day, unless
the Piper plays."

Karlo called through the gloom. "We'll sing

47

the sun up through the sky. So sing," he
commanded and they sang:

"*There is a land of sunshine and of snow...*"
Karlo called to them again: "Now! Look
behind you!"

Faint and pale, the first rays pierced the
mists. Around them rose the hills, and dim
and distant lay the valleys. Their shadows
raced before them.

Suddenly the marchers halted. They shivered, but from fear, not cold. Behind them a gigantic shadow blotted out the sun. A great figure stood there, pipe in one hand, sword in the other. The Piper played, and this time the sound did not comfort. It chilled their hearts.

A RESCUE

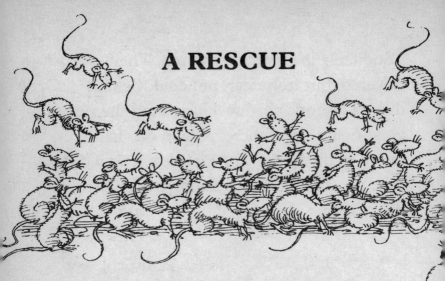

"Sing," commanded Karlo, and they sang. Their singing drowned the Piper's playing. In a rage he stowed his pipe in his belt and shouted: "Just you wait till I catch up! I promised you, lame boy, that I would have your blood, and so I will."

With huge strides, the Piper came towards them. The children stood, struck dumb with terror.

Then the strangest thing happened. From the rocks came a muttering and a rumbling. Rats came tumbling, leaping, great rats, small rats, black rats, brown rats. They flooded over the mountain tract and blocked the Piper's way.

And who should be at their head, but
Josefina and Mortimer? Both were silvery
grey, but as spry as ever.

The Piper raised his pipe and began to play
again. But Josefina taunted him:

"Here are your enemies, the rats
Bold as dogs and swift as cats
And, what's more vital, we're immune
To lying promise and deceitful tune.
So, go on, Piper, do your worst
Blow your pipe until you burst."

Grimly the Piper put his sword and pipe
away. He knew he was beaten. With clenched
teeth he watched the children march away.

HOMEWARD BOUND

They formed a long column, four by four. On either side ran the rats.

The sky smiled blue, and the sun shone on their faces.

Day by day they marched in cold, in heat, through flood and dust.

Karlo urged them on.

"If you are tired, find someone wearier, carry them on your back. If you're afraid, find someone who is scared and put your arm

round them. You'll feel bolder. And sing."

They sang, they marched. At night, when they fell by the road to rest, the bigger ones guarded the smaller, while Karlo and Mo and Jo guarded everyone.

Then the day came when the towers of the first city rose on the skyline. A child called out in wonder, "I know that place."

But as the marchers reached the gates, the guards on the walls above shouted: "Wait. We'll take as many children as you like, but not the rats."

Josefina turned to Karlo. "Now you must pay your debts. We helped you, and you must help us."

Karlo called up to the guards. "You cannot pick and choose. Together we have broken the Piper's spell. Now each town must have rats as well as children again."

They had to agree in that town and in every town. Day by day the marching column grew shorter, until one morning the smallest child cried out:

"I see a town, a river and a hill."

KARLO'S TOWN

The walls of the town were crowded with weeping, cheering people. But the gates were locked and no keys could be found. The Mayor had them.

"Where is that rogue?" demanded the Teacher.

Where indeed? The game was up for him. He was busy ransacking the town treasury, stuffing his pockets full of gold. He was spotted just as he left. The crowd gave chase. But though weighed down with plunder, the scoundrel escaped.

And the gates were still locked.

"Break down the gates," shouted the Cobbler. The guards smashed the locks, the huge doors swung open and the children, still singing, crowded in. The whole town rushed to meet them.

Parents cried: "We will be different. We'll share our joy and sorrow. We'll be kind and strict, fair and unfair too. But we'll never imagine we could do without you."

The children answered:

"We will be good, and bad as well. But we'll stick together. We'll never run away again."

The Cobbler looked down at their bare, travel-stained feet and said: "I'll make every one a new pair of shoes."

The Teacher said, "School at nine sharp tomorrow."

Karlo looked round for Jo and Mo. But not a single rat was to be seen. He grinned to himself. Tonight he'd leave two pieces of cake by his bed.

STRANGE MEETING

One summer evening in a village beer garden, a man dressed in scarlet rags sat drinking. His pockets were nearly empty. At the next table he saw another man the worse for wear dressed in tattered red and yellow.

"Off to a fancy dress ball?" he mocked.

The other grinned.

"You too? But wait. Don't I know you?"

The Mayor and the Piper stared at each

58

other. Of course they'd met before.

The Mayor said, "It's you, you rogue. I'll wager you can't show your face in any decent town."

"Nor you."

They embraced like brothers and drank each other's health. Then the Piper said,

"I'm off now. Here's to the future."

"What future is there for people like us?" asked the Mayor.

The Piper smiled, a wicked smile.

"While there are folk like you, my friend, there's room for people like me."

Josie Smith by Magdalen Nabb

Josie Smith lives with her mum in an industrial town; she is a resourceful, independent little girl who always does what she thinks best, but often lands herself in trouble.

Josie Smith at the Seaside
by Magdalen Nabb

Josie Smith makes friends with a girl called Rosie Margaret; with the donkey, Susie; and with a big friendly dog called Jimmie, who swims off with Josie Smith's new bucket.

Josie Smith at School by Magdalen Nabb

More muddles and misunderstandings for Josie Smith. She is horribly late for lessons when she tries to get a present for her new teacher. And then she helps her new friend to write a story and completely forgets to do her own homework!

Josie Smith and Eileen by Magdalen Nabb

Josie Smith doesn't always like Eileen because Eileen has things that Josie Smith longs for – a birthday party, a bride doll, and the chance to be a bridesmaid in a long shiny pink frock. But Josie is happy in the end.

GOOSEY FARM:
A DOG'S JOURNEY
Gene Kemp

"The summer we went to live at Goosey was magic – the sun seemed to shine all day long."

For the first time in their lives, Widget and her little brother Tim can roam about the hills and fields with their two dogs Russet and Dizzy Frizzy. And Sam the Boss Cat is never far away, usually waiting to pounce on Russet! After a shaky start – and a few scraps – Tim and Widget are making new friends. With the added excitement of puppies to look forward to, everything seems perfect at Goosey. But autumn brings change and, with the first sparkle of frost in the air, comes an unforgettable tragedy...

A heart-warming story from one of today's best-loved authors. Carnegie medallist Gene Kemp's exquisite writing brings a breath of country air to all young readers.

Order Form

To order direct from the publishers, just make a list of the titles you want and fill in the form below:

Name ....

Address ....

....

....

Send to: Dept 6, HarperCollins Publishers Ltd, Westerhill Road, Bishopbriggs, Glasgow G64 2QT.

Please enclose a cheque or postal order to the value of the cover price, plus:

UK & BFPO: Add £1.00 for the first book, and 25p per copy for each addition book ordered.

Overseas and Eire: Add £2.95 service charge. Books will be sent by surface mail but quotes for airmail despatch will be given on request.

A 24-hour telephone ordering service is avail-able to Visa and Access card holders: 041-772 2281